Illustrated Classics

FRANKENSTEIN

By
Mary Shelley

Retold for young readers
by D.J. Arneson

Illustrated by Eva Clift

Chapter 1
Frankenstein's Strange Secret

It was a dreary night in November. Thick fog filled the narrow cobblestone streets of the small Swiss town like smoke from a cheerless fire. The snow-covered Alps were shrouded in darkness. They hovered over the town like white-haired giants.

The yellow glow of a candle flickered in the attic window of a small house. Inside, a young man sat silently at his desk. He stared at an open notebook filled with writing. The final words glistened in wet ink. The man read them aloud.

"I, Victor Frankenstein, have discovered the secret of life," he said. He sat back in his chair and repeated the last words. "The secret of life!"

Frankenstein gazed out of the window into the night. Fiery streaks of lightning danced over the distant mountains. The flash illuminated the peaks and then died so that only the shadows of the mountaintops remained. He closed the notebook. "There is only one way to prove my discovery is correct," he said. "I must create a living creature. A human being!"

The man's face looked older than his years. Dark circles ringed his eyes and his skin was deathly pale. Dull black hair hung in limp strands over his forehead and down his neck. The only sign of his youth was a bright glow deep within his eyes.

Frankenstein put the notebook into the desk drawer and blew out the candle. He threw a cape over his shoulders and hurried downstairs. He paused before entering the street. He glanced in both directions. A stray

"I must create a living creature.
A human being!"

6

A graveyard lay behind the building.

dog trotted by and vanished into the fog. It was late. The town was asleep. "I must not be seen," he said. "People would not understand." He clutched his cape tightly to ward off the chill wind and stepped into the darkness.

A strange, sweet smell drifted on the wind as Frankenstein neared the outskirts of town. "The smell of death," he said. He stopped in front of a low stone building. It was the town morgue. It stood at the side of the road, isolated and alone, as if it held a dreadful secret. A graveyard lay behind the building. Hundreds of stone crosses and dozens of stone crypts lurked in the shadows.

The clanking and scraping of a shovel

7

broke the silence. Frankenstein listened. The unseen digger continued his work, unaware of his visitor. Frankenstein waited until the noise stopped. He watched as a flickering lantern emerged from the darkness. It seemed to float in the air as the digger, cloaked in darkness, carried it to the morgue.

Frankenstein slipped into the abandoned graveyard. He threw back his cape and looked down at the newly turned earth. "I cannot turn back now," he said. He began his grim task. He worked without stopping through the night.

The first rays of the morning sun peeked over the rim of mountains. The graveyard turned pale orange. Frankenstein glanced up from his work. "I must leave at once or risk being seen," he said. He closed the top of a large canvas sack at his feet. He tied it securely and hoisted it to his shoulders. Like a mouse stealing corn, he hurried from the graveyard and walked quickly down the street. He did not slow down until he reached his tiny attic room. He opened the lid of a large wooden chest and emptied the contents of the canvas bag into it. He locked the chest and fell on his bed, exhausted.

Someone knocked sharply on his door. "Mr. Frankenstein!"

Frankenstein opened his eyes. "Yes, who is

*Frankenstein emptied the bag
into the chest.*

it?" he asked.

"Mrs. Bruch," a woman's voice answered.
"There is a letter from your father."

Frankenstein crossed the small room and
opened the door just wide enough to see out.

"There is a letter from your father,"
Mrs. Bruch said.

An elderly woman greeted him. She handed him a white envelope. "The postman brought it this morning," she said.

"Thank you," Frankenstein said. He slipped back into his room and quickly closed the door. He tore open the letter and began to read.

"Dear Victor," the letter began. "I have not heard from you for many months, but I understand. I know how busy you are with your studies at the university. William is growing up to be a wonderful little boy. He will be five years old soon. Your dear friend, Henry Clerval, sends his greetings. And Elizabeth sends her love."

Tears welled in Frankenstein's eyes as he finished the letter. He folded it neatly and put

10

it on his desk. "My dear friends," he said. "How I miss you. Little William, my sweet little brother. Henry, my closest friend. Elizabeth, my love and future bride. And you, dear father..." He turned toward the chest. "My great wish is that you understand the importance of my work." He wiped his eye with the back of his hand. The town clock chimed two. Frankenstein turned to the single small window of his room. He looked out. "My wish is that the whole world will understand." He folded the empty canvas bag and tucked it under his arm.

Ten minutes later, Frankenstein arrived at the university. Students rushed like ants from building to building. Frankenstein clutched the bag to his chest and entered a gray building. The words "Medical School" were engraved in

"My wish is that the whole world will understand."

11

A dozen sheet-covered figures lay inside the dissecting room.

the stone arch over the door.

Frankenstein was no different from the other students at the university. He passed unnoticed down the quiet hall. He stopped at a door to listen. "The dissecting room is empty," he said. He turned the handle and entered.

The room had no windows. Hissing gas lamps flickered overhead. The young man's shadow danced eerily as he closed the door behind him and crossed the room.

A dozen bare tables stood in neat rows in the center of the large room. Their tops were solid slabs of white marble. Wooden cabinets covered the walls. Hundreds of shiny metal instruments glistened behind their glass doors. Medical knives, saws, and scalpels sparkled like jewels in the flickering gas light.

Frankenstein opened his canvas bag and placed it on a nearby slab. He stepped to a thick metal door at one end of the room. He pulled it open. Inside, masked in shadow, lay a dozen sheet-covered figures. They lay on large zinc trays like people in eternal sleep. Frankenstein went to work at once.

That night, Frankenstein returned to the graveyard. By morning, his canvas bag was heavy. He repeated his secret visits day after day and night after night.

Months of sleepless nights and sunless

"I am ready to begin."

days passed. Frankenstein's skin turned yellow. His eyeballs bulged from sunken sockets. His cheeks were hollow. But the bright light still shined from his eyes.

After many weeks, the dark chest in his room was full. He studied its strange contents. "Everything is here," he said. "I am ready to begin."

The young scientist faced his empty operating table and raised his upturned hands to his face. He grasped the air with his delicate fingers. "With these hands I will create life," he said. "When I have finished, my creation will rise from this table."

He set to work at once. He worked feverishly.

He mixed chemicals according to ancient methods he learned from rare books. He devised new formulas. He constructed a complicated maze of glass tubes.

The tiny attic room reeked with the smell of boiling chemicals. The room became as hot as a furnace. Sweat pored from Frankenstein's forehead. When an experiment succeeded, he moved on to the next. When he failed, he started anew.

A boiling hot bottle of bright red fluid exploded. Frankenstein wiped the foul-smelling stuff from his face. "I will not give up," he said. He rolled up his sleeves and mopped the mess from the floor.

"I will create human life," Frankenstein vowed. "I will not fail."

Chapter 2
The Monster Lives!

Many months later, Frankenstein approached the large wooden operating table that filled the center of his small room. Cheap wax candles surrounded the table. They sputtered noisily as he gazed at an immense, canvas-covered form lying on the table. The rough sheet covered the form from head to feet.

Frankenstein pulled back a corner of the sheet. He held a flickering lantern close to the thing on the table. "He is finished!" he exclaimed.

The thing was a gigantic human. The candles' uneven light threw strange shadows onto the walls. The thing on the table seemed to move, but it was only the dancing shadows. The thing was as still and silent as death.

Cold rain splattered against the room's tiny window. Blue flashes of far-off lightning illuminated the night sky. The mountain peaks glowed and then vanished in darkness. Hollow

booms of thunder rolled down the valley. Frankenstein went to the window and wiped the grimy glass. He put his face to the pane. He squinted sharply through the darkness to watch the distant lightning. "The spark of all life on earth," he said. A crisp smile crossed his lips. He turned to the table. Behind it, on his desk, stood dozens of bottles, vials, and glass tubes. A blue flame glowed under a large copper pot. Pipes and wires criss-crossed the desk. They filled one side of the room like a giant spider's web.

An explosive jolt of lightning turned the sky white. A roar of thunder shook the room. The jars and wires glowed orange. Sparks erupted from the copper pot. Sharp smelling smoke rose from the wires as they turned red with heat. The room filled with blue light. It grew brighter and brighter. Frankenstein threw his hands over his face to protect his eyes. The light was so bright it felt hot. Beads of perspiration covered his brow. "What have I done?" he cried.

As fast as it appeared, the light faded. The room was pitched back into murky darkness. Only the feeble candles gave light. Even the lightning stopped as the mountain storm ended as quickly as it started. The town went back to sleep.

"He lives!" Frankenstein shouted.

The room was cold again. Frankenstein turned slowly toward the table. He stared at the thing he had made. A corner of the canvas fell away from the face. By the glimmer of the half extinguished light, he watched the creature's dull yellow eyes open. "He lives!" he shouted. "My creation lives!"

The sheet draped over the immense form quivered. An arm slipped off the side of the table and hung loosely in the air. The arm rose. Frankenstein stared without blinking. The creature's chest heaved. He emitted a dry, hollow gasp as air rushed in to fill its lungs. Its

legs quaked. The table shook. The thing was alive!

Frankenstein rushed to the desk. He unhooked the tubes and wires connecting the creature to the bottle-filled desk. He ripped the wires away. He flung the tubes aside. He tossed the glass bottles and vials to the floor. He grasped the gray sheet covering his creation. He paused. "I have worked for two long years to bring you to life," he said. "I have done all in my power to make you beautiful. To make you perfect. I have selected each part of you in proportion with the others. I have taken infinite pains to create a being of utmost beauty." His hand quivered. The canvas fluttered. He tightened his grip. "Now! Behold my work. Behold perfection!" He tore away the canvas and looked square into the face of the giant he had made.

"AAAiiieeeee!"

Frankenstein threw his hands to his face. He covered his eyes and staggered backwards. He stumbled. The shattered bottles and vials on the floor rang like broken bells.

The creature sat up. His yellow skin scarcely covered his bulging red muscles. His arteries and veins clung to his limbs and body like crawling purple vines. Long, shiny black hair hung in coarse, uneven tufts from the top of his mammoth head. The pegs of square, pearly teeth shined through straight black lips in the dim candlelight. His rough skin was shrivelled like the skin of an over-baked potato. His watery eyes swam in red-rimmed sockets like birds' eggs floating in blood.

Frankenstein screamed. He threw his hand to his mouth in disgust.

The creature sat on the table like a trusting pet waiting for its master. A thin smile curved his black lips. His eyes blinked with hope. He raised an arm and opened his giant hand. He reached out for the man who had made him. His lips moved. "Uuunnngghh," he muttered, struggling to make his first sound.

"Nooooo!" Frankenstein screamed. "You are ugly!" He turned his back on the creature and ran out of the room.

Chapter 3
The Terrible Truth is Known

Frankenstein paced the town's streets all night. A red dawn began to break. Soon the sun would rise. He would have to face the truth. He clenched his fists and shook them in the air. "I have not created beauty," he uttered. "I have created a monster!"

People entered the street. Shops opened. The town came to life. Friends greeted one another with smiles and best wishes for a prosperous day. Women carried hot bread from bakeries to their homes. Later, small children scampered over the cobblestones on their way to school. Happiness filled the air. Nobody paid attention to the forlorn figure walking among them.

Victor Frankenstein was not happy. "I can never go back," he muttered. "I dare not face the horror of what I have done."

The clatter of horses' hoofs and the rumble

of iron-rimmed wheels broke the morning calm. A carriage approached. A man leaned from the carriage window. "Victor!" the man shouted. Frankenstein did not hear.

"Victor!" the man shouted a second time. "Victor Frankenstein, my dear, dear friend."

The voice was familiar. Frankenstein

Clerval stepped to the street.

turned as the carriage stopped nearby. The carriage door opened and the man stepped to the street.

Frankenstein put his hand to his chest in surprise. "Clerval!" he gasped. "Oh, Henry, my friend, how glad I am to see you."

Henry Clerval stared wide-eyed at his boyhood friend. They had grown up together, but Clerval scarcely recognized the gaunt man before him. Before he could ask what the trouble was, Frankenstein fell to the street, unconscious.

"Help me," Henry Clerval shouted to the carriage driver. The two men hoisted Frankenstein into the coach. Clerval read Frankenstein's address from a paper he carried in his pocket. In minutes, the men trudged up the stairs to Frankenstein's attic room with the unconscious scientist between them.

"Help me!"

25

Clerval pushed open the door. He winced as the sharp odor of electricity and chemical smoke stung his nose. He and the driver placed Frankenstein on his bed. The driver left.

"He is a monster," Frankenstein moaned. "Beware. A monster. He is my creation."

Clerval dropped to his knees at his friend's side. Frankenstein was delirious. His eyes were closed. Sweat poured from his brow. "You are ill, Victor," Clerval said. He wiped Frankenstein's brow. "You are having a nightmare." He covered his friend with a tattered blanket. "Now sleep," he said gently. "Sleep."

Clerval stood. He studied the room. It was in disarray. Broken bottles and chemical apparatus lay everywhere. A desk filled with wires and tubes reeked of chemicals. Clerval went to the window and forced it open. He glanced into the alley three floors below. A giant figure dashed around the corner. It vanished so quickly, the surprised Clerval barely noticed. He returned to the bed where Frankenstein slept. "I will stay by your side until you are well, my dear friend," he said.

Chapter 4
Friendless and Alone

Night fell over the town. A pale moon rose, but its light was cold and dim. A watchman paused on his rounds. A noise from the shadows caught his attention. He held out his lantern and peered into the darkness. "Is anyone there?" he called. The answer was silence. The watchman shrugged his shoulders and walked on.

The shadow within the shadow moved. A huge figure emerged from the darkness. It paused long enough to be brushed by a stray moonbeam.

The creature, a man of immense size, stared after the watchman. He reached out his hand as if asking to be touched. "Unnnhh," he muttered. The watchman was already too far away to hear.

The creature dropped his arm and hung his head. He was as wide as a door and over

The giant blinked away his tears.

eight feet tall. He was oddly dressed in clothes that scarcely fit. He shivered in the chill night air.

The giant looked over his shoulder at the small, three-story house at the end of the street. The warm glow of candlelight flickered from a small attic window. He blinked away tears as he watched the window for a very long time. It remained empty. He turned away and moved with remarkable speed to the edge of town. Within moments, he was deep inside the forest. He walked through the darkness until he reached a quiet clearing. He sat down, surrounded by loneliness, and wept.

The next morning, the sun rose with unusual brilliance. Its warm rays flooded the clearing. Nearby was a bubbling brook. The creature lay on the grass asleep. A bird chirped. The giant's eyes opened wide. A shiver of fear ran down his back. He sat up and glanced around. His hands shook and his teeth chattered from cold. He rose and the bird stopped its song.

The creature kneeled at the brook and drank. He picked berries from bushes that were heavy with bright red fruit and ate them. When he was full, he walked deeper into the forest. He forgot his fear. He listened to the birds. He watched the clouds drift overhead. He wrinkled his nose at the smell of grass, flowers, and moist earth. Each sight, sound, and odor sharpened his wakening senses. By

The creature kneeled at the brook and drank.

The fire was warm.

midday, his vision was crisp. His ears were keen. His nose missed nothing.

A bird lighted in a branch near the creature's head and began to sing. The giant reached for it. The bird continued its song. "Eeek, eek," the giant said, trying to imitate the bird. He smiled.

The creature lived in the forest for many weeks. One day he smelled smoke. He cautiously approached a clearing. Small flames licked from a hunter's abandoned campfire. The giant approached it carefully. He put his hand near the fire. It was warm. He smiled. The heat felt good. He put his hand into the glowing embers. "UNnnngh!" he roared. He jerked back his hand, wincing with pain. He was puzzled how something that gave pleasure could also give pain.

A pleasant smell rose from the fire. Part of a small animal, the remains of the hunter's meal, still roasted on the red coals. The creature picked it up and sniffed it. "Mmmm," he muttered. He put the meat to his mouth and tasted it. His thin lips curved in a smile. He popped the remainder of the meat into his mouth, bones and all, and ate.

The creature roamed the nearby woods for many days. He never got far from the fire which he fed with fresh wood. He ate berries and once in a while he caught a rabbit or a squirrel. He cooked the meat over his fire. Each day filled

"*Mmmm!*"

his mind with wonder. The rays of the sun warmed him, but night's cold shadows chilled him. Rain caused discomfort when it soaked him, but a drink of cold brook water refreshed him. The song of a bird gave him delight. Thunder and lightning terrified him. He was pleased by the beauty of the woods, but at night, he was very sad, lonely, and afraid.

One morning the creature awoke, shivering with cold. A thin layer of snow covered the clearing. He scooped a handful of the white stuff and smelled it. He tasted it. He shook his head, puzzled by what it could be. He turned with alarm toward his fire. It was out. He stared into the silent woods, not knowing which way to go. Food was already scarce. He shook the snow from his immense body and trudged deeper into the woods.

The morning sun soon melted the snow. A familiar smell drifted through the woods. It was smoke. The creature followed the scent. The smoke came from a shepherd's hut. He approached it quietly and looked in the open window. An old man sat by a fire cooking his breakfast. The creature smacked his lips and smiled. He pushed open the door and stepped inside.

The old man turned at the sound. His eyes bulged with fear at the sight of the giant

standing in his doorway. "Aieeee!" he screamed, "A monster!" He dropped his cooking pot and raced out the door.

The creature reached out for the man, but the man didn't stop running. Soon he was out of sight. The creature's brow furrowed. He shook his head sadly. He was confused. He put his huge hands to his face and ran his fingers over it. "Unnh?" he muttered.

The smell of cooking food overcame the giant's sadness. He ate from the shepherd's pot and left. He was no longer hungry, but his loneliness grew with each step.

That evening the giant came upon a small

village. A few simple huts and cottages lay snug against the base of the mountains. He approached one of the cottages with great caution. Voices and the smell of cooking came from the open door. The giant went to the cottage. He paused at the door and then entered.

A cluster of small children playing near the fireplace stopped chattering when the giant's huge shadow crossed the floor. They turned. The creature smiled at them. The children's faces turned ashen with fear.

"EEEeeeeee!" they screamed.

The children's mother entered the room. "A monster!" she screamed. She fainted to the floor.

The shouts rang through the village. A

The angry crowd closed in on the cottage.

dozen men and women ran toward the cottage.

"Something has happened!" a man shouted.

"Someone is attacking Frau Holz's children!" a woman cried.

"Help save them!" another man called.

Soon everyone in the small village was in the street. The men carried clubs and the women waved sharp knives. They gathered around the cottage. "Who is there?" a farmer with a pitchfork shouted.

The children from the cottage streamed out the door. "Monster! Monster!" they screamed. The crowd closed in on the cottage.

The giant emerged from the door. He blinked in wonder at the angry crowd. He smiled and held out his open hands to the villagers.

"Kill him," a woman shouted.

"Don't let him hurt the children," a man bellowed.

A barrage of heavy rocks flew from the crowd. They struck the giant on the head and chest. He threw his arms in front of his face to protect himself.

"Don't let him get away," the man with the pitchfork shouted.

The creature spun one way and then the other. There was nowhere to run. The angry crowd moved toward him waving their weapons in the air. The giant's mouth opened wide. "Uuunnnngghhh!" he roared. He flailed his arms as if the people attacking him were a flock of vultures and ran for his life.

"Don't let him get away," the man with the pitchfork shouted.

Chapter 5
A Home in the Woods

Winter lingered over the mountains and valleys. The giant roamed the woods, hurt and confused. He hunted for food at night and slept during the day to avoid people. He found a large piece of coarsely woven cloth in an abandoned hut. He threw it over his shoulders for a cloak to ward off the cold wind.

One evening the giant spied a light through the dark forest. Hungry and cold, he walked toward it. The light came from a small cottage in a clearing. The giant went to the window and looked inside.

A fire flickered brightly in the fireplace. A young girl stirred a pot hanging over the fire. An old man sat at a rough wooden table. The giant pressed his face to the glass. He felt the warm glow of the fire against his cheek. "Unnnh?" he moaned as he watched the happy scene.

The giant watched from the window.

A noise on the path alarmed the giant. He retreated into the shadows. A young man approached carrying a heavy load of sticks. He dropped the sticks by the front door and went inside. "I found enough wood for two days," he said proudly.

"Then we shall be warm for two days more," the girl said.

"Spring is not far off," the old man said. "Life will get better."

The giant understood none of it. He slipped back to the window. He watched as the girl put bowls on the table and filled them with steaming soup. The three people sat down and talked

41

*The creature pushed
the door open.*

cheerily as they ate. The muffled sounds were meaningless to the giant, but he understood the smiles.

The creature stood at the window for hours. He didn't turn away until the last candle was blown out and the family went to bed. He walked around the corner of the house to return to the woods. He stopped. A small wooden hut rested against the cottage. It was only half as tall as the giant. Its door was no higher than a sheep's back. The giant dropped to his knees. He pushed the door open and crawled in.

The little hut was dry. Except for a few small cracks, the walls were tight and kept out the wind. The giant closed the door. He pulled his knees to his chest and ducked his head so he could sit. He pulled his cloak over his shoulders and fell asleep.

A noise awakened the creature the next morning. He was cramped and stiff. He turned his head to a small crack in the wall between the house and the hut. He put his eye to the crack. He could see perfectly into the house without being seen.

The girl stirred the cooking pot. The sweet smell of hot porridge rose from the pot and drifted through the crack in the wall. The creature sniffed hungrily.

The door to the cottage opened. The young man entered with an armful of wood. He stacked it by the fireplace. "Agatha," he said to the girl. "Is father awake?"

"Yes, Felix," Agatha replied. "He is getting potatoes for our supper."

Just then the old man entered. He held two

sad-looking potatoes in one hand. In his other hand was a cane. Felix hurried to his side. "Let me help you, father," he said. He took the potatoes and led the old man to the table.

The giant squinted at the father's face. The old man's eyes were closed. He was blind.

"I don't know how we'll manage if spring doesn't come soon," Felix said.

The old man patted Felix's arm. "We have each other, my son," he said. "We will survive."

"I'll find work today," Felix said. "But I must also gather wood or we'll freeze."

"First, you must eat," Agatha said. She ladled a thick spoonful of hot cereal into a bowl and handed it to Felix. "Porridge," she said. She put a spoonful into another bowl and set it in front of the old man. "Porridge," she repeated.

The creature watched closely. He saw that what the girl was doing had something to do with the sounds she made. He listened as she spoke again. "More porridge, father?" she asked the old man.

The porridge's moist aroma filled the hut where the giant sat hunched over in front of the tiny crack. "Porrrdge," he whispered. "Poorrdge." From that moment on, he watched and listened so closely that it was almost as if he were in the room.

That evening Felix returned to the cottage. He carried a small bag. "Food," he said as he dumped the contents of the bag onto the table.

The giant watched. He moved his lips. "Food," he said softly.

Felix's face saddened. "I found work," he said. "But now we have only enough wood for tonight."

"I will gather the wood tomorrow," Agatha said.

"But you have to look after Father," Felix said.

The old man banged his cane on the floor. "I can look after myself," he said.

Agatha and Felix smiled.

That night as the family slept, the giant slipped deep into the forest. He gathered a huge arm load of wood and carried it to the cottage. He left it in a pile next to the door.

The sun was barely up when the cottage door opened. Agatha stepped outside. She was bundled against the cold. She carried a small axe in her hand. "Oh, my!" she exclaimed. She rushed inside.

The giant watched through the crack. Agatha pulled Felix to the door and pointed at the pile of sticks. "Wood," she said. "Enough for a week."

The giant moved his lips. "Wood," he said.

The giant left the pile of wood next to the door.

46

Chapter 6
"I Want to be Your Friend."

Spring arrived just as the old man promised. The giant stayed in his hut all day, watching and listening. At night he gathered berries for himself and wood for the family. Sometimes he caught a rabbit which he placed by the door.

Each day the giant added more words and ideas to his life. At night he listened as Felix read books to his father. He learned about lands beyond the mountains. He learned about oceans. He learned to think and to speak. But as much as he learned, he had no friend. He was as lonely as the farthest star.

The family did not understand their good fortune. "We must trust Providence," the old man said. The others agreed.

The creature looked longingly through the crack. "I want to tell them it is me," he said softly, "but I am afraid."

The old man sat in the kitchen playing his violin.

Later that morning, Agatha and Felix were outside tending the family's small garden. The giant peeked through the crack. The old man sat in the kitchen playing his violin. "I must have a friend," he said softly as he listened to the music.

The creature touched his face. He patted the rough skin with the tips of his giant fingers. He ran them through his coarse hair. "People run when they see me," he said, "but Father cannot see. Maybe he will be my friend."

The giant put his eye to a crack that let him see outside. Agatha and Felix worked side by side in the garden. "I will wait until they go to the market," he said. "Then I will talk to Father. I will tell him I am the one who gathers wood and catches rabbits for them. I will tell him I want to be their friend. He will understand.

When the children come back, he will tell them I am their friend, too. We can live together and be happy."

The giant waited day after day. Then, early one morning, he heard Agatha and Felix talking. He put his eye to the crack in the wall.

"We are going to the market, Father," Agatha said.

"We will sell the vegetables from our garden and hurry back," Felix said.

The old man patted his children on their shoulders. "Don't hurry," he said. "I can take care of myself."

Agatha and Felix kissed the old man on the cheek. Agatha brushed a stray lock of gray hair from his forehead. She picked up a bundle of dew-covered vegetables and Felix slung a bag over his shoulder. They went out the door and were soon out of sight.

The giant trembled. His hands shook. His knees quaked. "I want to be your friend," he said quietly. His voice was rough and dry. He practiced the words again. "I want to be your friend," he repeated. The sound was raspy, like the growl of a sleepy tiger. He glanced through the crack into the kitchen. The old man played his violin. Its music was as sweet as Agatha's voice when she sang. The giant swallowed hard. He pushed open the door of his tiny hut

51

"I want to be your friend."

and stepped into the sunshine.

Violin music poured from the open kitchen door. The giant walked silently up the path. He stopped in the doorway. The music stopped suddenly.

"Is someone there?" the old man asked.

The giant started to turn around. He stopped and faced the old man. "I am a traveler," he said. "May I stop for a rest?"

The old man put his violin on the table. He smiled. "You are welcome in my house, my friend," he said.

The giant blinked back a tear at the word

"friend." He stepped inside the cottage.

"I am blind," the old man said, "but you may help yourself to what little we have."

The giant pulled a chair away from the table. He sat down. "I would only like to talk," he said.

The old man smiled. "That's wonderful," he said. "I have my children, but I do get lonely for a new voice now and then."

The giant settled in his chair. A smile played over his thin lips. "I want to be your friend," he said.

The old man reached for the giant. He found his arm and patted it warmly. "That's wonderful," he said. "I'd like to be your friend,

too."

The giant's lips opened wide in a grin as big as a peapod.

The old man started to talk. He talked about his life. He talked about Agatha and Felix. He talked about the mysterious provider who gathered wood and food for them. He talked about everything under the sun. The giant took in every word as if they were drops of honey.

Suddenly, the old man stopped talking. "Listen!" he said. "My children are returning." His keen hearing picked up the sounds of footsteps long before they reached the giant's coarse ears.

The creature stood up so quickly he knocked over his chair.

"What is the trouble, my friend?" the old

"Don't forsake me."

man asked.

The giant's mind was in turmoil. "I must tell him who I am," he thought. "He will tell the children I am his friend and they will not be afraid. I must do it now." He dropped to his knees and grasped the old man's legs. "I am the one who gathers your wood," he said. "It is I who puts rabbits and berries by your door. I want to be your friend."

The old man sat back in alarm. "Who are you?" he cried.

"I am your friend," the giant said. He began to sob. "Don't forsake me."

Felix grabbed a heavy stick and leaped at the giant.

Felix entered the cottage. Agatha was right behind.

"Father!" Felix shouted at the sight of the giant clutching the old man by the knees.

The giant turned his head to face the children.

"Aaaaaiiieeeee!" Agatha screamed. She

fainted to the ground.

Felix dropped his bag. He grabbed a heavy stick resting by the door and leaped at the giant. He raised the club and beat him mercilessly.

The giant could have torn the youth limb from limb. Instead, he stood. He held off the blows with his arms, but he did nothing to stop them. Tears poured from his eyes. "I want to be..." He did not finish. A sharp blow struck him on the head.

"AAAAAARRRRRGGGHHHHHHHH!!!!!!"

The giant rose to his full height. He threw Felix aside with a powerful blow of his arm. He leaped over Agatha who lay unconscious on the path.

"AAAAAARRRRRGGGHHHHHHHH!!!!!!" he bellowed. His booming voice thundered up and down the valley. He turned his back on the cottage, the terrified old man, and everyone else and ran into the forest.

The giant raced through the woods. He flailed his arms. He struck out at anything that got in his way. He roared like a wounded lion. He didn't stop until he reached the top of a towering mountain. He faced the valley below. The setting sun hung over the mountains behind him. His gigantic black shadow stretched across the valley to the far horizon.

"AAAAAARRRRRGGGHHHHHHHH!!!!!!"

"I am hated!" he screamed. "I am reviled!" He raised his powerful arms high over his head. "As much as the world hates me, I will return that hate a thousand times!" The thunder of his voice rolled across the land. He scanned the horizon. "I will start with the man who created me. Frankenstein!"

The creature ran down the hill at lightning speed. His power was greater than any mortal man's.

Chapter 7
The Monster's Revenge

It was early summer. People strolled happily through the public park outside of Geneva. A bright, orange and black butterfly fluttered across the dark green grass. It lighted briefly on a flower and then flew again.

"A butterfly," a little boy exclaimed. He chased after the tiny creature. The butterfly weaved and bobbed through the air like a leaf on the wind. It drifted into the nearby woods. The little boy followed. Soon he was far off the beaten path. Shadows filled the forest. The air was chill. The butterfly flew into the darkest part of the woods. It landed gently on top of an enormous dark form lying on the ground.

The little boy stopped in his tracks. He stared at a huge dark figure lying in the shadows. The little boy's eyes opened wide. His mouth fell open. The form moved.

The creature's yellow eyes opened slowly.

He saw the boy. A thin smile crossed his lips. He rose to his knees. The boy froze. The giant stood up. He towered over the boy like a tree over a bush. He reached for the boy.

"Be my friend," the creature said. His low voice rumbled coarsely.

The boy quivered with fear. "Get away from me," he cried. "You're ugly. Go away!"

The giant grasped the boy. "No," he pleaded. "I have suffered enough. I wanted revenge, but that is past. I won't harm you. Come with me. Please, be my friend."

The little boy stared into the creature's misshapen face. "You are a hideous monster,"

The giant put the boy on the grass.

he shouted. "Let me go or I will tell my father. He is an important official in Geneva. Everybody knows Judge Frankenstein."

The giant's eyes widened. His thin lips parted. "FRANKENSTEIN!" he roared. It was the name he reviled. The hate that time had healed returned. In its place was revenge.

The child struggled. The giant placed his enormous hand around the boy's neck. He tightened his grip. The boy's arms fell limp. His eyes closed. He was silent.

The giant put the boy on the grass. "I swore revenge against my creator," he bellowed. "It has begun!" He grabbed a locket hanging from the boy's neck and ran into the depths of the forest.

The sun's last rays faded as evening

approached. The creature stopped at a small barn not far from where the boy's body lay. "I will hide here until it is time to strike again," he said. He entered the barn. He glanced at a pile of straw heaped in the corner. A young girl lay on it, sound asleep.

The creature walked quietly to the girl's side. He gazed down on her. Her face glowed with the innocence of a child. The giant's hatred softened. "Could you be the one to love me?" he whispered. The girl sighed, but did not awaken. "I would give my own life for just one look of love." He shuddered as he realized the truth of his strange life. "No. It can never be," he said. "If she wakens, she will be like the others and denounce me."

The giant held up the locket so it caught the sun's dying light. A cruel smile crossed his lips. "I will not be the one to suffer, " he said. "You will!" He put the locket into a pocket of the girl's skirt. "I will still have my revenge!" He ran from the barn.

Chapter 8
Tragedy Strikes...Again!

Victor Frankenstein rose from his bed. He was thin and weak, but his long illness was over. He was fully recovered. Clerval had nursed him for many months. Now his dearest friend was gone.

Frankenstein crossed his small room to the door. An envelope protruded from under the door. He picked it up and tore it open. He smiled. "Ah! A letter from Father," he said. He read the letter's first line. His face turned ashen. "NO!" he screamed. "It can't be true. My dear little brother is dead! William has been murdered in the park."

Frankenstein threw the letter to the floor. He pulled a satchel from beneath his bed and stuffed it with clothes. "I must go to Geneva at once," he said. "Father and Elizabeth need me." He ran down the stairs.

By nightfall, the carriage bearing Victor

Frankenstein reached the park at the outskirts of Geneva. He raised the carriage curtain and peered through the gloom. "Stop!" he shouted to the driver.

The carriage stopped. Frankenstein climbed out. He took his bag and walked toward the park. The carriage continued into the town.

Lightning filled the air with electricity.

"William has been murdered!"

An immense figure loomed like a shadow.

Thunder roared in the heavens. A cold wind blew Frankenstein's cloak. He pulled it tightly to his chest. He stopped. "It was near here the innocent child was murdered," he whispered. "I can feel it."

A hideous laugh answered him from the shadows. A brilliant flash of lightning turned the night into day. Frankenstein whirled toward the laughter. An immense figure loomed like a living shadow among the trees. "YOU!" Frankenstein screamed. "You are the murderer!"

The split second of light was gone. The

"Victor, my son!" Judge Frankenstein exclaimed.

park was pitched into inky darkness. Frankenstein dropped his bag and ran toward the spot where the creature stood. Another bolt of lightning sizzled overhead. The giant was gone.

Frankenstein retrieved his bag and went straight to his father's house. "I will tell all that I know," he said as he rang the heavy bell. "My creation killed William, and I am the murderer!"

Judge Frankenstein opened the door. "Victor, my son!" he exclaimed. He threw his arms around the young man standing in his door. "You have been away at the university for three years. Now you return to this."

Elizabeth appeared behind Judge Frankenstein. "Victor, my love," she cried.

Victor embraced Elizabeth. The three wept openly.

"The murderer has been caught," Judge Frankenstein said.

"He has?" Victor exclaimed.

"He?" Elizabeth said. "It is not a he, Victor. It is Justine, our trusted servant."

Victor put his hand to his forehead. He staggered. "But I am the..."

His father interrupted. "She was found near the place William was murdered," he said. "The locket he wore was in her possession."

"It must be some mistake," Victor said.

*"Victor, my love,"
Elizabeth cried.*

Elizabeth shook her head. "No, dear Victor," she said sadly. "It is the truth. She confessed to the crime this morning at her trial."

Victor staggered again. He felt faint. He recovered his composure. "Where is she?" he asked. "I must speak to her at once."

Judge Frankenstein led his son into the house. "She is in the jail," he said. "She has been sentenced to hang."

"No!" Victor shouted, "that cannot be." He turned back to the door. "I am going to the jail."

Frankenstein burst out the door. He ran down the street and did not stop until he arrived at the Hall of Justice. He entered. "I must see Justine Moritz!" he said to the jailor.

"I will take you to her," the jailor said.

Frankenstein followed the man down the huge stone hall. Their footsteps clattered noisily. The jailor stopped in front of a large iron door. "The murderess is in here," he said. He unlocked the door.

A young girl of 18 sat in the somber cell. A peaceful smile lighted her face. "Mister Frankenstein!" she said quietly. "How happy I am to see you."

Frankenstein took the girl's hands. "They said you confessed to William's death, Justine," he whispered so the jailor could not hear. "I know that is not true. Why did you confess?"

Justine smiled. "My confessor told me that was the only way to save my soul."

"But you didn't do it," Frankenstein said softly.

Justine's smile spread over her whole face. Her eyes brightened as if they were glowing candles. "It is enough that you know I am innocent," she said serenely. "I am at peace."

"But..." Frankenstein stopped.

"There is nothing you can say or do," Justine said. "I am ready."

"You have to leave now, sir," the jailor said.

Frankenstein embraced Justine, but he could not speak.

The next morning, long before the cock crowed, the town bell rang thirteen times. Its mournful song spread over the town like a shadow of gloom.

Frankenstein paced the empty streets. He had been there all night long. As the bell's final chime died into silence, he covered his face with his cape. "She is gone," he said. "And I am guilty of another murder."

Chapter 9
Frankenstein Meets his Monster

The two deaths weighed heavily on Frankenstein. He sat alone in the garden of his father's house for days. Elizabeth was troubled. She went to him. "You must forget these tragedies," she said. "I cannot let my future husband become ill."

Frankenstein's father entered. "Elizabeth is right," he said. "Clerval tells us you nearly died last winter. Get some rest, Victor. Look after your health and your future."

Frankenstein looked into the distance. "You are right," he said. "I'll go to the mountains. They brought me joy when I was young. Perhaps I can find peace there again."

The next morning Frankenstein saddled a horse. He threw a pack over the animal's back. Elizabeth and Judge Frankenstein were with him. Frankenstein hugged Elizabeth. "Our wedding will be joyous," he said. He mounted

"I remember this place well."

the horse and turned the animal toward the street.

By mid-afternoon, Frankenstein reached the base of the mountains. He transferred his pack to his own back and began to climb. By early evening he was above the timberline. His destination, a mountaineer's hut on top of a steep cliff overlooking the valley, was still high overhead.

Frankenstein reached the hut as the sun began its final descent. He dropped his pack inside the door and went to the edge of the cliff. The rugged mountains stretched as far as the eye could see. Below him, covering the deep valley like a giant carpet, was a glacier. It was already in shadows. "I remember this place well," he said. "I sat here as a child and..." He stopped suddenly. Something moved across the top of the glacier. It was the figure of a man. It moved with incredible speed.

Frankenstein's jaw dropped. "It cannot be!" he exclaimed.

The figure raced over the glacier. It leaped to the rocks and began to climb. Within minutes it was at the precipice. A giant hand appeared over the edge. It was quickly followed by another. The creature's head appeared. He pulled himself onto the precipice.

Frankenstein threw his hands over his face. The creature's ugliness was too horrible to see. "You! Foul devil!" he cried. "How dare you approach me."

"HA HAH HAH!" the creature roared. "You, my creator!" he mocked. "How dare you turn your eyes from your own creation!"

"I did not want to create evil and ugliness," Frankenstein shouted.

The giant shuddered with rage. "Look at

me, Frankenstein," he cried out. "I am your creation!"

Frankenstein uncovered his face. His eyes widened as he studied the giant's cruel features. "Why are you here?" he asked. "Is it to kill me?"

The giant threw open his huge cloak to reveal his immense body. "It would be too easy," he said. The cloak flapped noisily in the wind like the broad wings of a gigantic bird.

Frankenstein drew back. A shiver of fear shook his spine. "Then why have you followed me?" he demanded.

The giant's thin black lips curved to a faint smile. "I will never leave you," he said. "Unless..."

Frankenstein leaped forward. His rage drove him like a mad man. He plunged headlong

"I am your creation!"

"Don't think you can get rid of me so easily."

into the giant's chest. One push would send him over the edge. The mammoth creature did not budge.

"Don't think you can get rid of me so easily," the giant said. "I have learned to love life. I will not give it up now."

"You are a fiend!" Frankenstein screamed.

"Because you made me so," the giant answered. "You gave me life and life has rejected me. I am excluded from love and companionship. My misery has made me a fiend."

"I can't do anything about that," Frankenstein answered.

The giant's scowl softened. "Yes, you can," he said. His voice grew calm. "Make a companion for me."

Frankenstein blinked. "A companion?" he said.

"Give me a mate."

"Yes," the creature shot back. "A mate who will share my life with me."

Frankenstein folded his arms across his chest. "Never," he spat. "Another creature like you would only double the evil I have made."

The giant's eyes glistened with tears. His lips quivered. "No," he said. "I promise. Give me a mate. A wife. Do this and I promise we will never threaten mankind again. We will go to the farthest place on earth where ordinary beings cannot survive. We will live in peace. I swear it."

The creature's plea touched Frankenstein. "You swear it?" he asked.

The giant's face brightened. "Yes!" he

"Both of you will retreat to the north."

shouted. "Yes, yes, I promise."

Frankenstein remained silent for many minutes. He paced back and forth between the hut and the creature at the edge of the precipice. He stopped and faced the giant. "I will do it," he said. "I will make a woman for you on one condition."

The giant leaped forward with joy. "Yes, anything," he said. "I will do it."

Frankenstein pointed over the mountains to the distant north. "When I deliver a wife to you, both of you will retreat to the north," he said. "You will stay there forever. You will never return."

The creature dropped to his knees. "Yes," he said. "I swear it by the sun and the sky." He rose slowly to his feet. His eyes darkened. His face hardened. His voice was firm. "I will never be far from you," he said. "I will be watching and waiting. I will know when your work is finished and I will be there."

The giant being whirled and in two steps was over the precipice.

Frankenstein ran to the edge. He looked down at the glacier hundreds of feet below. The creature raced over the frozen ice like the wind and vanished among the shadows.

Chapter 10
"Be Watchful!"

Frankenstein returned to Geneva the next day. He paused in front of his father's house. His heart was heavy. "I dread the thought of creating another living being," he said, "but I must. My life is worthless if I fail." He pushed open the door.

"Victor! Dear friend!" Henry Clerval greeted him with a bright smile. "I am here with a wonderful idea. Join me on a trip. We will visit all the great cities of Europe."

"Yes," Frankenstein replied. "It is a wonderful idea."

The two old friends immediately made plans for a grand tour of Europe. But Frankenstein had a second plan he did not discuss with Clerval. "I will use this trip as an excuse to begin my grim task," he thought. "I will collect what I need to make the creature's mate. I will take it to a remote place and do my awful work. Nobody will know what I have done."

The departure day arrived. Elizabeth and Judge Frankenstein stood by the carriage that would take the men away. The judge took Victor and Elizabeth by the hand and joined them. The two young lovers faced one another. "When you return, Victor, you and Elizabeth will be joined in marriage," the judge said.

"I will wait patiently, my love," Elizabeth said.

"I look forward to our happiness together," Victor replied. His voice was edged with sadness.

"Does something trouble you, Victor?" Elizabeth asked.

Victor forced a smile. "No! No, my love, it is nothing," he said.

Clerval leaped into the carriage. "Come, Victor, life awaits us!" he shouted. "Let our adventure begin!"

The two men leaned from the carriage window as it rolled out of sight. "I will return to you soon, my love," Victor shouted. "Be patient. Be watchful."

Clerval sat back in the carriage. He gave a quizzical look at Victor who sat across from him. "What did you mean, 'Be watchful?'" he asked.

Victor slumped in his seat. He waved off

"Does something trouble you, Victor?"

Victor left for Scotland.

the question with a brush of his hand. "Nothing, my friend," he replied. "I meant nothing at all." He put his hand to his forehead and began to think.

"I fear for the lives of Elizabeth and Father," he thought. "They are unprotected from the demon. He could hold them hostage until my work is complete. If I don't fulfill my task quickly enough, he might harm them. How can I know if I am I doing the right thing?"

The thoughts troubled Victor, but he soon gave in to Clerval's enthusiasm. Two months passed rapidly. The two young men visited famed cathedrals and libraries. They saw ancient castles. Each city they visited carried Victor farther from his unwanted task. But he never forgot. He secretly collected the things he would need to create another being.

Six months passed. The two friends were in London when a letter arrived for them. "It is from our friend Hugh Lockwood," Victor said as he read the letter. "He has invited us to visit Scotland."

Clerval shook his head. "You go alone," he said. "I have too much to do here. When you return, we'll continue our adventure."

"This is the opportunity I need to do my work," Frankenstein thought. He put his hand on Clerval's back. "Done," he said. "I will leave immediately."

"Take as much time as you need," Clerval said. "I will be here."

Chapter 11
Another Monster!

Frankenstein left immediately for Scotland. He did not go to his friend's estate. Instead, he went to a small town on the coast at the northernmost end of the country.

"I want to hire a boat," he said to a fisherman at a secluded dock.

"What kind of fish are you after?" the fisherman asked.

"I just want a boat," Frankenstein said sharply.

The fisherman scratched his head. "Just askin'," he said. He pointed to a heavy rowboat bobbing in the bay. "Will that do?"

"It will do just fine," Frankenstein said. He piled his trunks and boxes into the boat and climbed in.

"Any idea where you're going?" the fisherman asked. The bay was covered with fog. The sea beyond was invisible.

Frankenstein reached a desolate island.

"The Orkney Islands," Frankenstein said. He dipped the boat's oars into the water and rowed into the fog.

"Keep it straight if you can," the fisherman shouted. "With luck you'll hit them. If you don't, you'll be back on the foam."

"On the foam." Frankenstein said. "What does that mean?"

The fisherman shook his head. "Your body'll wash up on the beach like foam," he said. "Good luck."

Frankenstein rowed through the night. The fog cleared enough to steer by the stars. By morning the small boat was beached on the remote shore of a desolate island. "This is where I will do my work," he said. He unloaded

the boat and walked inland.

The island was little more than a wind-swept rock. The soil was barren. The sound of waves pounding the shore reached every corner. A few cows grazed on stunted grass. A half dozen people lived in a group of stone huts in the island's center. It was a place with very little life.

Frankenstein pounded on the door of a hut. A bearded man opened the door a crack and peered out. "I need lodging," Frankenstein said.

The man looked at the well-dressed young man is if he were a prize cow. "Pay in advance," he said. He pointed to a low hill more than a mile away. Fog hung on the hill. A tiny hut poked its roof through the top of the fog like an outcast.

"Done," Frankenstein said. He handed the man a sum of money.

The man eyed Frankenstein's pile of chests. "I'll help carry those if you like," he said.

"No!" Frankenstein snapped. "Don't touch them."

The man scowled at Frankenstein. He stepped back into his hovel and slammed the door.

Frankenstein dragged and carried his chests to the hut. He kicked open its door. The door sagged on its hinges. The inside was barely liveable. Plaster fell from the walls. The thatched roof had gaping holes. There was no furniture. "There is no place on earth as far

A tiny hut poked through the fog.

87

away as this," he said. "My secret work will remain my secret."

Frankenstein hired the bearded man to repair the hut. He bought a few simple pieces of furniture. Two weeks after he arrived, the place was liveable. One room served as his quarters. The other was his laboratory.

Frankenstein opened the chests. They contained his strange collection of chemicals, glass tubes and jars, and shiny copper wires. He left two large chests of other things unopened. He assembled the instruments. He sharpened the scalpels. He joined the wires and tubes. The work took many weeks. "It is finished," he said late one night. "My laboratory is complete." The room was a replica of his old laboratory. He stepped outside.

A fresh wind blew against his cheek. The fog that normally hung over the house drifted away. The beach and the black sea were visible for the first time. Candlelight flickered in the windows of the huts below. Other lights on nearby islands glimmered like fireflies over the sea. Frankenstein's hands began to shake. "I cannot do it!" he said aloud. "I cannot create more evil." He went to bed. He was greatly troubled.

The fog was back the next morning.

Frankenstein opened his chests of strange laboratory equipment.

Frankenstein awoke. He entered his laboratory. He opened the remaining chests. He sighed heavily. "I have no choice," he said. "I must do it."

The young scientist set to work. He spent each day from morning to night in the laboratory. Slowly, the creature he already despised took shape. Its size was equal to the giant's. It filled two tables. The arms and legs were enormous. The body was immense. Everything was in proportion, but the measure was gigantic. The work took many months.

At last, only one step remained. "I am nearly done," Frankenstein said. "Now it is time for nature to do its work." He stepped outside. The night was dark. Thick fog hung over the hill. He studied the sky. A pale yellow moon appeared through black holes and then

Only one step remained.

disappeared. "A storm will give it the spark of life," he said. "When it comes, I will be ready."

A hollow laugh echoed through the fog. Frankenstein whirled toward it. The laugh came again, this time from behind him. He spun to face it. The laugh echoed again and again, each time from a different direction. Frankenstein stepped quickly into the hut and slammed the door. He went straight to the laboratory.

The blue flame of his burner sputtered beneath bottles and vials. Boiling chemicals coursed through criss-crossing glass tubes. A bubbling sound filled the room. The lifeless form lay on the table as silent as death.

"Heh, heh, heh."

The laughter sounded again. Frankenstein

The monster peered in the window.

spun to face the window. A huge face peered in. It was the creature. His giant red eyes stared longingly at the enormous figure lying on the table. His thin black lips curved to a ghastly grin.

"You!" Frankenstein screamed at the creature. "You have been watching me for all of these months." He spun to face the lifeless giant on the table. His disgust returned. "And you!" he shouted. "You lie there waiting for life. But, how do I know you won't be evil? What promise is there you won't hate him? How can I know if you will go in peace or if you will turn against me?"

Frankenstein paced the room. He tore his hair. He shook his fists. "If you are evil, all future generations will suffer," he cried. He

"How do I know you won't be evil?" Frankenstein shouted.

The giant howled with despair.

went to the table and gazed at the giant, lifeless woman. "He told me the two of you would retreat to the north and never return," he said. "But you have promised nothing. You may be more evil than he!" He spun and pointed a sharp finger at the creature staring through the window.

Frankenstein leaped onto the table. He dropped to his knees. "I will not do it!" he screamed. He tore the lifeless form to pieces with his bare hands and scattered the bits across the room.

"AAAAARRRROOOOOOOOGGGHHHH!"

The giant at the window howled with despair. His cry echoed across the island. He stared into the room, wide-eyed with disbelief. He watched helplessly as the creation his future depended on was destroyed. He glared at Frankenstein with unequaled hatred. "AAARRRRGGGHHHH!" he roared.

Frankenstein slammed the laboratory door and bolted it. He waited. "He will come for me now," he said.

The creature's tormented wail melted into the night. Silence covered the island like fog. Frankenstein opened the door. The creature was gone. He was alone.

Frankenstein stumbled to his room and fell into bed. He closed his eyes but he could not sleep. Each rumble of distant waves stirred his mind. Each mournful moan of wind filled

Frankenstein bolted the laboratory door.

him with fear. He listened to the silence. "What's that?" he gasped.

The steady crunching sound of heavy footsteps approached the lonely hut. It stopped at the front door. The door creaked open and the footsteps continued to the door to his room. Frankenstein sat up with a start. The door burst open. The creature leaped into the room.

"You have broken your promise," he roared. "I waited and watched you all these months. My heart filled with hope. I cherished the day I would have a mate. A friend." He approached the bed. He pointed his enormous gnarled finger at Frankenstein's face. "You have destroyed my hope."

"Devil!" Frankenstein screamed. "I created you, but I will not create more evil. Be gone!"

The monster gnashed his teeth. "You created me," he howled, "but I am your master. I am fearless and powerful. I will never leave you."

The giant glared at Frankenstein with bulging red eyes. His black mouth opened wide. His thick tongue quivered like a cornered rat in its hole. "I will be with you on your wedding night," he hissed. He turned to the door and stepped into the darkness.

Frankenstein ran to the doorway. The sky was clear. The fog was gone. He stared down the hill to the beach and the sea below. A rowboat shot over the waves with the speed of an arrow. It headed into a thick blanket of fog lying low on the water and disappeared. The monster was gone.

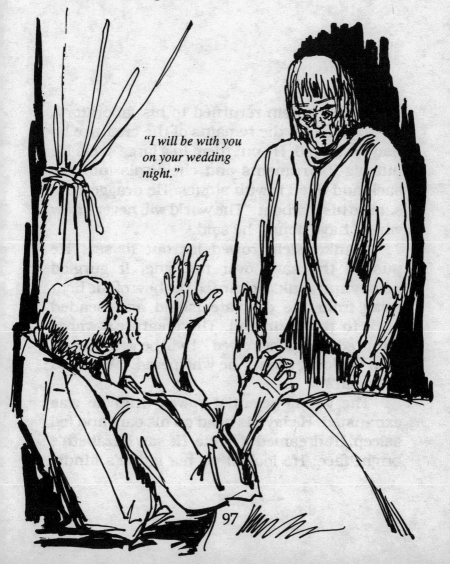

"I will be with you on your wedding night."

Chapter 12
The Creature's Curse

Frankenstein returned to his laboratory. He scooped up the remains of the creature he had destroyed. He put them in a large sack. He put his instruments and chemicals into the sack and filled it with stones. He dragged the sack to his rowboat. "The world will never know what I have done," he said.

Frankenstein rowed far out to sea. He pushed the sack over the side. It gurgled noisily and sank. He turned the bow of the boat away from the desolate island and headed back to the mainland. The creature's words haunted him as he rowed. "I will be with you on your wedding night," he whispered. "What did he mean?"

The young scientist rowed until he was exhausted. He lay his head on his oars and fell asleep. He dreamed of home. He saw Elizabeth's bright face. He looked on his father's kindly

"The world will never know what I have done."

"Come with me, sir."

smile. He saw Clerval's happy grin. He slept fitfully until a faint shout awakened him.

The boat drifted close to shore. A group of people on the beach waved at him. "Come ashore," a man called.

Puzzled, Frankenstein rowed ashore. The man stepped to his side. "Come with me, sir," he said.

"And why should I?" Frankenstein replied.

"The magistrate wants to see you?" the man said.

"Magistrate?" Frankenstein said. "I have broken no laws. Why does he want to see me?"

"A young gentleman was murdered here last night, sir," the man said. "That is all I can say."

The crowd moved away as the man led Frankenstein from the beach. They walked to the nearby town and entered a low building. The magistrate, a somber, gray-haired man greeted them.

"Can you tell me the meaning of this?" Frankenstein asked the man.

The magistrate looked Frankenstein up and down. "A young man was found murdered on our shore last night," he said. "He was strangled."

"Well, I can assure you I had nothing to do with it," Frankenstein said.

"Perhaps not," the magistrate said. "But witnesses saw a boat with one man in it near the scene. He rowed away with great speed before he could be identified."

"It was not I," Frankenstein said. He was upset to be a suspect in a terrible crime.

The magistrate put his hand to his chin. "Our investigation has just begun," he said. "Now, would you kindly view the body?"

Frankenstein shrugged his shoulders. "If it will please you," he said. He followed the magistrate to a room at the back of the building. The room's windows were draped. It was dark and dreary. A table stood in the center of the room. A body, covered by a white sheet, lay on

"Who has he killed this time?"

the table.

The magistrate stepped to the table. "This is not a pleasant sight," he said. "The murder was brutal. The marks of the killer's fingers are still black on the victim's throat."

The words struck Frankenstein like a blow. He staggered backward. The memory of

William's murder flashed through his mind. "The monster!" he thought. "Who has he killed this time?"

The magistrate threw back the sheet covering the body. "Henry!" Frankenstein screamed. His eyes rolled back into their sockets. He gasped for breath and fell to the floor. The body was Henry Clerval.

Frankenstein was carried to a room with barred windows. "He will have to stand trial," the magistrate said. "His actions lead me to suspect he is the murderer."

Chapter 13
The Curse...Fulfilled!

Three months passed. Frankenstein lay deathly ill. At last he was well enough to stand trial.

The courtroom buzzed with excitement as Frankenstein entered. "He's the one," a man whispered. "He murdered his best friend," a woman said. "He'll hang for it," another man said. Everyone nodded.

The judge took his place at the head of the room. The door at the rear opened. It was the magistrate.

"Your honor," the magistrate said, "I have a statement to make."

The judge wagged his finger at the magistrate. "Let's hear it," he said.

The magistrate faced Frankenstein. "I have looked after the accused these many months since his arrest," he said. "He was delirious and spoke strangely. Fortunately, I understood him. He said many things. I investigated all his wild statements…"

"Yes, yes," the judge interrupted. "Get on with it. What is it you want to say?"

The magistrate held up a sheet of paper. "Victor Frankenstein was on the Orkney Islands when his friend's body was found," he said. "This paper is signed by witnesses. He could not have committed the crime!" He thrust the paper on the judge's desk.

The crowded courtroom burst with shouting. The judge read the paper. "This case is dismissed," he said over the excited voices. "Victor Frankenstein is innocent. He is a free man!"

Frankenstein left immediately for Geneva.

The magistrate held up a sheet of paper.

"Victor Frankenstein is innocent!"

He spoke to no one. His mind was filled with gloom. "I am the real murderer," he said to himself. "I am to blame for William's death and Justine's execution and now..." He choked with emotion. "And now I have caused the death of the best friend I ever had." He threw his hands to his face and wept.

The creature's face appeared in his mind. The monster laughed openly. "I will be with you on your wedding night," he said.

Frankenstein tore his hands from his face. "You dare mock me!" he shouted. "I created you. I will destroy you!"

A week later, Frankenstein's carriage arrived in Geneva. Elizabeth and Judge Frankenstein met him. Elizabeth ran to him and threw her arms around him. "Oh, Victor, my love," she said. "Never leave me again."

The creature's face appeared in Frankenstein's mind.

"I have a dreadful secret to tell you."

"Never!" Victor exclaimed.

The old judge put his arms around the young couple. "We have endured tragedy," he said. "Now is a time to rejoice. You have the rest of your lives to be happy. Mine is soon over, but your marriage will wash away all our sorrow." The judge walked up the path to the house.

Elizabeth beamed. "I am so happy, Victor," she said. She looked up into Frankenstein's face. Her smile vanished as if she saw death. "What is it, my love? What is troubling you?"

Frankenstein held Elizabeth by the arm. "I have a dreadful secret to tell you," Frankenstein said.

Elizabeth stopped. She put her hands to her cheeks. "What is it, Victor? Tell me," she said.

Frankenstein stroked her forehead and smiled. "No, my love," he said. "It must wait until after we are married."

"But..."

Victor put his fingertip to Elizabeth's lips. "Say no more," he said. "I will tell you, when you are my wife."

A magnificent wedding was planned. The happy day arrived at last. The ceremony was held on the judge's estate. Throngs of friends and well-wishers filled the grounds. Victor and Elizabeth were wed beneath a flower-covered arbor. The judge stood at their side.

"Isn't she beautiful?" a woman whispered to her companion.

"He is so handsome," another said.

The crowd murmured its approval of the young couple. The ceremony ended. Victor and Elizabeth embraced.

"This is the happiest moment of my life," Elizabeth said.

Frankenstein smiled. "And mine," he said.

The judge hosted a splendid party for the newlyweds. Then, as the sun began to sink, Victor and Elizabeth hurried to a waiting

The happy day arrived at last.

carriage.

"Where are they going for their wedding night?" a woman asked the judge.

The judge beamed. "They have a small property on Lake Como," he said. "They will spend their first days of happiness there."

Restless horses pranced on the gravel drive. Victor and Elizabeth waved from the carriage window. The carriage pulled away.

The carriage arrived at Lake Como late that night. Victor carried Elizabeth into their small house on the shores of the lake. The carriage left and they were alone.

"I have never been happier," Frankenstein said.

"I, too," Elizabeth sighed. "But you promised to tell me your secret."

Frankenstein's smile disappeared. "The time is not right," he said. He glanced around the room. The couple's trunks were where the driver left them. Frankenstein opened a small case. Inside was a pistol.

Elizabeth gasped. "Why have you brought a gun?" she asked.

Frankenstein was not listening. He looked around the room as if he expected to see someone he knew. He clutched the pistol tightly in his hand.

A shutter creaked. "What was that?"

Victor carried Elizabeth into their small house on the shores of the lake.

113

Frankenstein whispered.

Elizabeth laughed. "Only the wind, my darling," she said.

"Wait for me here," Frankenstein said. He went to the door and stepped out of the room.

"I know my enemy is here," Frankenstein said to himself. "He knows I have vowed to destroy him. Now is the time."

Frankenstein searched every room. Each one was silent and empty. He stopped outside the last. He raised the pistol and burst into the room. It was as vacant. He relaxed. "Can it be that he fears me?" he whispered. "Has he

Inside the case was a small gun.

114

forgotten his vow, or has he chosen to leave me in peace? Perhaps I..."

"EEEEEEEEEEEEEEEEEE!!!!"

Frankenstein's eyes widened with fear. His mouth dropped open.

"EEEEEEEEEEeeeeee..."

The scream ended suddenly.

"Elizabeth!" Frankenstein screamed. He raced down the hall. The room where Elizabeth waited was silent. He threw open the door.

"NOOOOOOOOO!!!" he cried.

Elizabeth lay on their wedding bed. Her wedding veil covered her face. The mark of the fiend's murderous black grasp circled her neck. She was dead.

"HAHAHAHAHAHA!"

Frankenstein whirled. The monster stood

in the open window. He flashed a square-toothed grin that filled his evil face. "HAHA-HAHAH!" he roared.

Frankenstein raised his pistol. He fired. A blast of flame erupted from the pistol. Black smoke filled the room. The smoke cleared. The window was empty. The monster was gone.

After Elizabeth's funeral, Frankenstein returned to his father's house in the same carriage that he and his bride rode on their wedding day. His face was hollow. Dark rings circled his eyes. He walked stiffly up the path.

A servant hurried to Frankenstein's side. "We received your sad letter," he said. "The news of Elizabeth's death has brought more tragedy to this house."

Frankenstein paused. He raised his face to the sky. "Is it Father?" he asked.

The servant nodded. "Yes," he said. "The shock was too great. He has died."

Frankenstein hung his head. He had no more tears left to cry. "My life is meaningless," he mumbled.

The monster's face appeared in his foggy mind. "Heheheheh!"

Frankenstein whirled. "Where is he? Where is the demon?" he shouted.

The servant looked around. "There is nobody here, sir," he said.

"You choose to live, do you?"

Frankenstein ran inside. He went to his room and threw himself on his bed. His rage rose like a wind-driven fire. He sat up. "I will find the beast and destroy him!" he screamed. "Let him feel my suffering. Let him feel my pain."

"Hahahahaha!"

The giant stood at the window. It was not a dream. It was the demon himself. "You choose to live, do you?" he laughed. "Then I am satisfied." He leaped from the window and ran into the adjoining woods.

"I will find you and destroy you!"

Frankenstein ran from the house. "I will follow you to the ends of the earth," he screamed. "I will find you and I will destroy you!"

"Hahahahahahahahahhahahah!" The fiend's hideous laughter died on the wind.

Chapter 14
The Monster's Last Victim...?

Captain Richard Walton stood on the deck of his icebound ship. The craft was far north of the Arctic Circle. It was frozen into the ice and had not moved since fall. Now it was spring. Lookouts scoured the bleak horizon day after day for signs that the ice would break up soon.

"Captain!" the lookout at the top of the mast shouted. "Someone is out there!"

Walton ran to the rail. He shielded his eyes against the icy glare. Far off on the ice was a small black speck. It grew larger. It was a sled pulled by a team of powerful dogs. An enormous man sat on the sled. He cracked a long black whip over the dogs' backs. "Great Scot!" Walton exclaimed. "What is he doing out there? And who is it that could be so immense?"

The sled drew closer. Walton put his telescope to his eye. He could just make out the form of the sled's driver. "He is a giant!" Walton gasped.

The rail crowded with men. They stared at the distant speck as it passed by. It grew smaller and disappeared over the horizon.

That night Walton recorded what he had seen in his logbook. The next morning he returned to the rail. This time a welcome sight greeted him. Large black cracks split the ice into giant rafts. "We'll be free, soon," he said to his first mate.

The mate stared at the ice. "Sir!" he said. "There's another sled."

Walton leaned over the side. A hundred yards away was a dog sled. The dogs pulling it

"Sir! There's another sled!"

"He's in bad shape."

were so thin their bones showed. They struggled, but the sled barely moved. A man lay huddled in furs on the sled. He held a whip, but it was motionless.

"Get him aboard," Walton ordered. A crew of strong sailors clambered over the side.

A few minutes later the man from the sled lay in Walton's quarters. The ship's doctor tended him. "He's in bad shape," the doctor said.

"Who on earth could he be?" Walton asked.

The man on the bed opened his eyes. They

were sunk deep in their sockets. He opened his parched mouth. "I am Victor Frankenstein," he gasped.

"Rest, man!" the doctor said.

Frankenstein raised himself on the bed. "No, I cannot stop now," he gasped. "I have seen him. I am close."

Walton leaned over the raving man. "Seen who?" he asked.

"The demon," Frankenstein said. "He is out there." He fell back on the pillow. "Help me to destroy him."

"I am Victor Frankenstein."

123

Frankenstein told his incredible story.

"The giant on the ice?" Walton asked.

"Yes," Frankenstein said. "That's him. The demon. My creation." He grasped Walton's hand. "Listen to my story, then you will understand."

Color returned to Frankenstein's cheeks. His eyes brightened. He even managed a smile. "It was a dreary night in November," he began. The words flowed faster and faster. He told the entire, incredible story. Captain Walton sat by Frankenstein's bed scribbling notes of everything his strange guest said.

Frankenstein described each detail of his

star-crossed life. His eyes welled with tears when he spoke of William's murder. He broke down and wept when he told how Clerval had died. He wailed loud and long when he mentioned Elizabeth and her cruel fate. He sobbed as he told of his father's death.

"I have destroyed them all with my creation," Frankenstein whispered. "I have vowed to track him to the ends of the earth to destroy him. I have followed him for endless months. Each time I get close, he escapes. But yesterday I saw him. He is out there."

Suddenly the color ran from Frankenstein's cheeks. His eyes grew dim. His head dropped to his chest.

"He is dead," Walton said.

Late that night Walton stood alone at the ship's rail thinking about Frankenstein's strange story. "I don't know to believe him or not," he said.

"HAHAHAHhahaha!"

A fiendish laugh broke the calm. It came from the room where Frankenstein's body lay. Walton ran across the deck to his cabin. He opened the door. His mouth fell open and his eyes bulged wide. A giant creature stood over Frankenstein's body. He was so tall he had to stoop to fit under the low ceiling. He turned to

A giant creature stood over Frankenstein's body.

the captain.

A devilish grin split the creature's twisted face. "Here is my last victim," he said. "Frankenstein created me and then abandoned me to unhappiness. Now it is ended."

The creature sprang to the cabin window and was soon borne away by the waves and lost in darkness.